Mouse's Christmas Cookie

by Patricia Thomas

illustrated by John Nez

two lions

Amazon Publishing
Attn: Amazon Children's Publishing
P.O. Box 400818
Las Vegas, NV 89140
www.amazon.com/amazonchildrenspublishing

Library of Congress Cataloging-in-Publication Data is
available upon request.

ISBN-13: 9781477847046 (hardcover)
ISBN-10: 1477847049 (hardcover)
ISBN-13: 9781477897041 (eBook)
ISBN-10: 1477897046 (eBook)

Book design by Vera Soki
Editor: Margery Cuyler

Printed in Mexico (R)
First edition
10 9 8 7 6 5 4 3 2

two lions

"Yummm!
Here's my Christmas dinner!"

...jingle, jingle, jingle!

Scritch,
scritch,
scritch...

"Dash away, dash away, dash away, all."

"STOP, MOUSE!"

"STOP, MOUSE!"

Scitter, scitter, scitter...

"MERRY CHRISTMAS, MOUSE!"

"Merry Christmas, Cat."